MOVE OVER!

Other Brockbank's

ROUND THE BEND
UP THE STRAIGHT
OVER THE LINE
MANIFOLD PRESSURES

MOVE OVER!

with Brockbank

CHANCELLOR
PRESS

To

All the women who ever married (even for a short time) chaps who go on like this.

ACKNOWLEDGEMENTS

The illustrations on pages 46 and 47 are reproduced by kind permission of the Proprietors of *Punch*. Of the rest all but one, on page 23, originally appeared in the pages of *The Motor*, to whose publishers the artist is indebted for permission to reproduce them.

First published in 1962 by Temple Press Books Ltd.
This edition published in 2003 by Chancellor Press,
an imprint of Bounty Books, a division of
Octopus Publishing Group Ltd,
2-4 Heron Quays, London E14 4JP

ISBN 0 7537 0846 9

FOREWORD

WHEN a family conference was called to decide a title for this book the secretary of the meeting (who is also treasurer and cook) immediately suggested "MOVE OVER" and the thing was done, for in the seven years since my last book of this kind the paramount change for motorists has been that there were getting to be too many of us.

The usual risk of a title getting out of date during the run of a book can hardly arise with this one—unless in a year's time none of us have room to move in any direction.

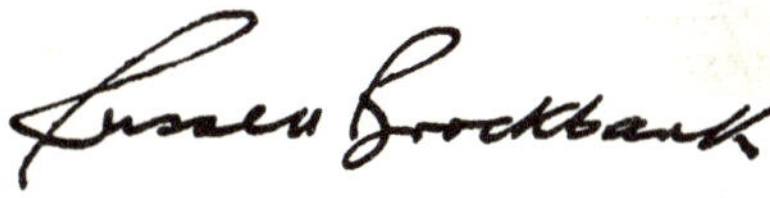

INTRODUCTION

Scratch a passer-by and you stand a good chance of finding a motorist—a thought which dawned on Russell Brockbank as long ago as the year of the first zebra crossings, when he had a London bus howling to a panic halt with four horrified top-deck passengers pushing their four right feet through the front panelling in sympathy. It was always one of my favourites. The other was a newspaper placard announcing: FOG IN CHANNEL—CONTINENT ISOLATED, which also came from the early post-war years when the jungle began at Dover. In those days the artist himself was an observer without a car of his own. Now he is one of the most enthusiastic and travelled motorists I know; if you can think of any unlikely, baffling, hair-raising, frustrating but instantly *recognisable* motoring situation, in or out of Britain, it is practically certain that Brockbank has either done it or has it on the drawing-board.

Don't ask me how he keeps up the flow. Twice a week for *The Motor*. almost as often for *Punch* he sees the things that happen to all of us and are usually funnier when they happen to somebody else. If you are not a regular reader of either magazine you can hardly have failed to see, in a certain oil company's mammoth signs, the same touch of an artist who admits to the "social vice" (I quote one of our cultural Sunday newspapers) of enjoying fast cars. Or old cars. Or any cars which have personalities as distinct and eccentric as their owners, and that covers most of the wheeled population on this side of the Atlantic.

RICHARD BENSTED-SMITH
Editor of "The Motor"

TO THE
MOTOR
RACES
Brockbank

The Keen Motorist will ensure he has Adequate Means to Warn of his Approach . . .

"What do you mean you've never heard of one that goes 'AOOGHA' "?

. . . and he (or she) will expect others to provide theirs . . .

"Shut up a minute, can't you?"

BEWARE
SUDDEN
AIRCRAFT
NOISES

He must learn to live with Mini-cars as best he can . . .

SUPPORT BALLET
LEFT HAND DRIVE
SUPPORT BALLET
LEFT HAND DRIVE
P
P

. . . whether he owns one . . .

. . . or not.

"Oh, NO!"

The Motoring Associations will help him all they can . . .

"Yours, I think."

. . . and so will the Police . . .

. . . and Passers-by . . .

"What kind of favour?"

. . . and, of course, Garages.

"Two gallons, please, and do you have any of that special oil that undoes rusty nuts?"

. . . and so will Road Signs — Official . . .

30
40
40
50

PASS
EITHER
SIDE

Boom
BEND
LUDC
BEND
L.U.D.C
Brockbank
BEND
LUDC

. . . and Un-official.

WORCESTER CATHEDRAL
MASS IN D

BREAKING IN

But he must still be prepared to Look After Himself . . .

. . . and his Faithful Steed.

As a Pedestrian . . .

. . . 10 . . 9 . .

. . 8 . . 7 . .

. . 6 . . 5 . .

. . 4 . . 3 . . 2 . .

. . 1 . . .

. . . or Passenger, he feels particularly Vulnerable.

"Your fast cab to London Airport, sir."

. . . *FIRE!*

"According to my fountain pen we're above 6,000 feet."

Animals are a Menace . . .

. . . or (in some circumstances) a Calculated Risk.

So are Snow & Ice —. . .

and Foreign Visitors . . .

LOWER
WEEDING

Brockbank

And Commercial Vehicles . . .

AND Motor Shows . . .

"It's for you!"

DINGBAT SPRING CO. LTD.
SALES

Brockbank

As though we hadn't enough troubles, THE COMMON MARKET is upon us, and our manufacturers may well find themselves making things they never made before — such as . . .

Dennis Brothers
a
Formula Junior —

— General Motors (U.K.) a Formula 1 —

— Lotus a Petrol Tanker —

— & Rolls-Royce
a
Bubble Car.

To get away from it all, the motorist turns to MOTOR RACING

"*Looks like they lightened the car considerably.*"

Long Distance stuff. . .

56
Brockbank

UILE Z
Brockbank

. . . and Short.

"I want a good clean fight, no butting in the clinches. I want you to break when I say break. O.K.? Then go to your cars and come out fighting."

"I remember seeing S. F. Edge going twice that speed in a car that cost half the money."

Club Racing has its Tribulations . . .

and its Rewards . . .

. . . but it is in the Grand Prix that the utmost is demanded of men and machines . . .

. . . and those who only stand . . .

. . . and wait.

No sooner has one season come to its close . . .

"The tragedy is that by the time they got the car built all the short drivers had signed up elsewhere."

. . . than preparations begin for the next.

"We don't reckon to be caught napping by the next *Formula 1."*

A WORD ABOUT RALLYING

There was once a chap lucky enough to WIN A NEW CAR in a "DAILY MAIL" COMPETITION. The only condition was that he drive it to Monte Carlo (in company with two experts) in the Rally at the conclusion of which it would be formally handed over to him.

Having made it plain from the start that he was NO EXPERT DRIVER—

—he went along purely in his private capacity—

—to keep an eye on—

—what (with luck)—

—or navigator—

—as a supervisor of looms—

—in a textile factory—

—would be—

—all his at the finish.

As for Foreign Touring . . .

"I would have sworn it leaned the other way."

. . . it's always nice to get HOME.

Finally, there are The Ladies . . .

THANK YOU
CALL AGAIN

"How does it know how much change to give me before I've put my money in?"

Brockbank

Brockbank

"Has my little girl done something foolish?"

. . . and Improvements generally.